Chuckie nervously twisted the hem of his T-shirt. Angelica said they only got one chance. He had to think fast, before the first shooting star fell.

Chuckie shoved his glasses up on his nose and rubbed his face.

Think, Chuckie, think! But the harder he tried to think of that one perfect wish, the less he could think of any kind of wish at all.

I've *got* to think of something before—

Rugrats Chapter Books

Chuckie's Big Wish

Based on the TV series *Rugrats*® created by Arlene Klasky, Gabor Csupo,
and Paul Germain as seen on Nickelodeon®

SIMON SPOTLIGHT
An imprint of Simon & Schuster Children's Publishing Division
1230 Avenue of the Americas, New York, New York 10020

Manufactured in the United States of America

First Edition   10 9 8 7 6 5 4

ISBN 0-689-82895-0

Library of Congress Catalog Card Number 99-73827

Chuckie's Big Wish

by Cathy East Dubowski
and Mark Dubowski
illustrated by Jose Maria Cardona

Simon Spotlight/Nickelodeon

Chapter 1

"This is the bestest adventure since Christmas Eve!" Chuckie whispered. Chuckie and Tommy were excited! Tommy's dad, Stu, was driving them, and Didi and Dil, to Beaver Lake.

Tommy nodded. It was way past their bedtime! "It's even betterer!" Tommy said. "This time we're *s'posed* to be awake!"

It was August, the time of the Perseid

meteor shower. That meant there were lots of shooting stars in the sky. Stu had come up with a great idea.

"We should take the kids out to Beaver Lake to see it," he'd said to the other grown-ups. "It'll be fun . . . and educational."

Everyone liked Stu's idea. It meant keeping the kids up past their bedtime, but at least it was for a good cause. A lot of the grown-ups had never seen a meteor shower before—or even a single shooting star. So now they were all headed to Beaver Lake. Angelica, Phil, and Lil were riding with Angelica's dad, Drew.

After a while, the cars turned off the main road and onto a gravel, tree-lined road.

Tommy peered out the window at a dark forest. "This would be a great hideout for Reptar!" he said.

Reptar was the scariest, neatest dinosaur that ever walked the earth. And he had his own TV show. Tommy and Chuckie had Reptar everything—Reptar toys, Reptar coloring books, Reptar toothbrushes, and Reptar pajamas!

Chuckie even had a Talking Reptar—a battery-operated model of the dinosaur that bared its teeth and roared when you squeezed its tummy.

Talking Reptar was Chuckie's pride and joy.

"I wish I had Talking Reptar with me now," Chuckie whispered to Tommy. "In case there are any scary monsters in the dark woods."

"Yeah," Tommy agreed. "Reptar would scare 'em away for sure."

The air coming in through the windows was cool and damp. Gravel crunched under the tires. Finally they stopped at a place with no trees. It was Beaver Lake!

Didi Pickles let Tommy and Chuckie out of their car seats. They clambered down while Didi unbuckled the strap holding Dil's car seat. Then she lifted the seat out by the handles, like a basket.

Dil made baby noises. It sounded like he was gargling.

"Can Dil say anything yet?" Chuckie asked Tommy.

"Not yet, Chuckie, but he's sure tryin'!" Tommy said. "Yesterday he tried all night!"

"You mean *cried* all night!" Chuckie said.

"That's what my dad called it. But I know he was tryin' to say somethin'!"

"I wonder what he meaned," Chuckie said. Dil made a noise that sounded like a cat with its tail caught in the door.

"That means he's happy," Tommy explained.

Angelica, Phil, and Lil walked up to Tommy and Chuckie.

"I think it means he's about to throw up," Angelica said. Her flashlight shone in Tommy's and Chuckie's eyes.

"Yeah, or maybe it means he's gonna mess his diapie!" Phil chimed in.

"Yeah, mess his diapie big time!" added Lil.

"Oh, yeah?" Tommy shot back. He covered his eyes from the flashlight beam. Tommy didn't like it when they made fun of his baby brother. "I bet his diapies are cleaner than yours!"

"Okay, okay, never mind about diapies. I hope you babies have been thinking about what you're going to wish for," Angelica said.

The babies looked at her, puzzled.

"Angelica," Tommy said. "What are you talking about?"

Angelica rolled her eyes. She couldn't believe how dumb these babies were! Lucky for them they had a big girl like her around to explain things.

"Don't you babies know anythin'?" she scoffed. "Why do you think we were dragged out here in the middle of nowhere in the middle of the night?"

Tommy, Chuckie, and the twins looked at one another.

"To see the pretty stars?" Tommy guessed.

Angelica laughed. "Do you really think the grown-ups would drive *all* the way out here just so you could see pretty stars?"

Tommy shrugged. "Sure, this is fun!"

"Tommy," Angelica said patiently, "we're talking about grown-ups. Grown-ups don't do anything unless they get something for it."

Tommy gave her a blank look.

"You know, like money!" Angelica said. "That's why they go to work every day—so they can get lots and lotsa money!"

She pointed to the sky. "Stars are going to shoot out of the sky and—"

Chuckie's eyes grew wide. "You mean money's gonna come out of a star?"

Angelica sighed. "No, no, no . . ." she began to say. Then she suddenly got an idea.

Angelica leaned forward and whispered in a deep, mysterious voice. "What I'm gonna tell you is super-super secret. I'm gonna be nice and tell you babies, but you can't tell anyone else."

The babies nodded their heads as they gathered closer.

"When you see the first shooting star, make a wish," Angelica continued, "and your wish will come true!"

The babies gasped.

"Why, you can even wish for lotsa monies!" Angelica added with a sly smile. Then she had one last thing to say: "Now I've been really, really nice to tell you this special secret, so you *have* to promise to give me some of the money, I mean, whatever you wish for."

"Uh, okay, Angelica," Tommy said. The other babies nodded their heads again.

Tommy and his friends were excited—they were going to make wishes!

Chapter 2

"Do you believe what Angelica said?" Chuckie whispered to Tommy. "About the shooting stars?"

The babies were following the grown-ups' flashlight beams down a trail from the parking area. They were heading to a beach where they could see the whole sky. Stu and Didi led the way, followed by the kids, then the other grown-ups.

"There *are* a lot of stars in the sky,"

Tommy whispered back.

"I know, Tommy," Chuckie said. "Do you believe they can make your wish come true?"

"Well, Angelica says they can," Tommy said. Angelica was a big kid and she knew a lot of stuff.

"Yeah, but have you ever wished on a birthday cake?" Chuckie said. "You know, first they light the candle. Then you're s'posed to make a wish. Then you blow the candle out. And if it blows out, you're s'posed to get your wish. . . ."

"Yeah, I know," said Tommy. "Your wish is s'posed to come true—as long as you don't tell anybody what it is."

"Well? Did you ever get your wish?" Chuckie wanted to know.

Tommy thought about it. "I dunno," he said honestly. "I can't remember what my wish was."

"Me neither," Chuckie said with a sigh. "I wish I could remember."

"Shh! Don't say 'wish' 'less you really mean it, Chuckie!" Tommy warned him.

They toddled down the trail in silence after that. An owl hooted in the distance. The air cooled as they hiked closer to the water.

When the families got to the beach, the grown-ups spread some blankets out on the ground and set up folding chairs.

"Have a seat now," Didi told the kids. Tommy and Chuckie sat together.

Then Stu stood up. He ran his hand through his hair as he waited for everyone to get quiet.

"Now, kids," he said, "what we're doing here is looking up, in the sky, at something called the Perseid meteor shower."

"Another name for what you are about to see is 'shooting stars,'" Grandpa Lou said. "They look like streaks of light in the sky. Reminds me of the Battle of the Bulge. Why, there I was, enemy fire whizzing over my helmet . . ."

Stu and his brother, Drew, exchanged a look. They had heard this story at least a thousand times.

"Uh, thanks, Pop," Stu said. "We'd love to hear about that . . . some other time." He smiled down at the children. "Now, keep your eyes on the sky, okay?"

The babies paid close attention. By the sound of Stu's excited voice, they could tell something big was going to happen!

Chapter 3

Stu pointed toward the sky, and the kids looked up, up, up . . . until, laughing, they fell over backward on the blankets. It was like lying in bed with the roof gone.

There was no moon tonight. So the stars sparkled like spilled sugar across the black sky.

"Okay, babies, get your wishes ready," Angelica whispered. "The firstest star is the lucky one! It's your only chance to make a wish!"

Oh, no, Chuckie thought. Only one wish, and mine isn't ready yet!

"Hey, Angelica," Chuckie asked softly.

"Quiet!" Angelica hissed. "You wanna make us miss the whole thing?"

Chuckie gulped. "Sorry," he whispered. "I just—"

"Shhhhhhh!"

Chuckie bit his lip. He looked over at Tommy, Phil, and Lil. They were all staring straight up and looking hopeful.

Except for baby Dil. He was asleep. Aw, he looks cute, Chuckie thought.

Dil opened one eye, as if he'd heard Chuckie's thought. "Ooh, ooh," he cooed.

"Hi, Dil," Chuckie whispered softly, so Angelica couldn't hear. "Are you gonna make a wish, little guy?"

Dil burped loudly, then fell back to sleep.

Chuckie glanced nervously at the sky. How much time did he have? He looked at the others.

I wonder what they're gonna wish for?

Angelica will probably wish for a castle with a ten-car garage, he thought. And maybe forty-'leven new Cynthia dolls.

And Tommy will wish for a Talking Reptar like mine.

Chuckie nervously twisted the hem of his T-shirt. Angelica said they only got one chance. He had to think fast, before the first shooting star fell.

Chuckie shoved his glasses up on his nose and rubbed his face.

Think, Chuckie, think! But the harder he tried to think of that one perfect wish, the less he could think of any kind of wish at all.

I've *got* to think of something before—

"Yeahhhh!" everybody yelled.

"What a beautiful shooting star!" Didi cried.

The noise woke Dil. He jerked and threw his rattle.

Bonk! It thumped Chuckie in the head. He looked up. A ribbon of brilliant white light arced across the night sky. Graceful and glowing and silent.

Chuckie quickly made a wish. And then the star was gone, like a birthday candle blown out.

The parents turned to one another, beaming. "Did you *see* that!?"

"It was *huge!*"

"I couldn't believe it!"

"Amazing!"

Angelica sat up and turned to the babies. "I hope you guys made your wishes!" she said.

All the babies nodded. Everyone, that is, except Chuckie.

"Chuckie . . . ?" Angelica said. She eyed him suspiciously.

"Yes, Angelica?" Chuckie croaked.

"Did you make a wish?" she asked.

Chuckie ducked his head. "Yes, Angelica," he mumbled. But the troubled expression on his face didn't go away.

There was something weird about Chuckie's wish. Angelica could *feel* it. She asked again, "Did you wish right when you saw the shooting star? Or was it after it was over?"

"Uh—" Chuckie began.

"It won't come true if you waited till it was over, you know," warned Angelica.

"I did it right, Angelica. Promise!" Chuckie said.

"Well, I hope so," she said. Then she lay back down on the blanket to look at the stars.

Chuckie had made a wish just as Angelica had told him to. And now his wish amazed him because it was so weird.

Why did I do it? Chuckie worried. Why did I wish for a baby brother?

Chapter 4

Chuckie woke up and squinted. Where am I? he wondered.

He looked around. Talking Reptar gazed back at him from the nightstand. Chuckie was in his room, in his own bed. But he didn't remember how he'd gotten there.

The last thing he remembered was his dad carrying him to the car. He had been feeling sleepy from looking at all the stars. . . .

And then he remembered: my wish!

Chuckie sat up. He pulled his covers up to his chin. He didn't hear anybody. He glanced around the room. He didn't see anybody. He reached for his glasses and put them on. He still didn't see anybody.

At last Chuckie got up the nerve to look under his bed. Nobody there. He looked in the closet. In the dirty-clothes basket. In the toy box. No one was there, either. Chuckie was alone.

"Where is my new baby brother?" Chuckie asked out loud.

Chuckie and Tommy screamed with delight. Reptar was baring his flesh-ripping teeth and roaring on TV.

"Reptar is the bestest dinosaur in the

whole wide world," Tommy said.

"Yeah, he sure is, Tommy," Chuckie agreed.

It was later that morning. Chuckie's dad had dropped him off at Tommy's house to play.

Chuckie raised his Talking Reptar to the TV screen and squeezed its tummy. Chuckie's Talking Reptar roared back at the Reptar on the TV screen.

"Can I . . . ?" Tommy asked, his eyes on the toy.

"Sure," Chuckie said. He hugged the stuffed dinosaur, then handed it to Tommy. Chuckie didn't let just anybody play with his Reptar. But Tommy was special. Tommy was his bestest friend.

Tommy squeezed the dinosaur's tummy. It roared back. Tommy giggled happily at the sound.

Then a toy commercial came on.

"*Roar!*" The commercial was about Talking Reptar!

"Wow . . ." Tommy sighed.

I bet that's what Tommy wished for! Chuckie thought. A Talking Reptar, just like mine.

The kids on the commercial bared their teeth and roared, "AWWRRRRR! Talking Reptar!"

"Did your wish come true yet, Tommy?" Chuckie asked when the commercial was over.

"I don't think we're s'posed to talk about it," Tommy said.

"What about *after* it comes true?" Chuckie continued. "Can we talk about it then?"

Tommy scrunched up his face. "I guess so—when it comes true, it'll be here. We'll hafta talk about it then."

"Can it disappear—you know, after it

comes true—if we tell anybody that it was our wish?" Chuckie wondered. He wanted to tell Tommy about wishing for a new baby brother. But he was too scared.

"I hope not," Tommy said. "Wait till you see mine! You'll be real surprised!"

Chuckie smiled. Tommy was the one who was in for a big surprise.

And maybe his dad, too.

Chapter 5

Angelica was fuming.

"It's been forever, Cynthia!" she said to her doll. "I wish my wish would hurry up and come true!"

Angelica had come to Tommy's house with her dad. Drew needed to pick up the lawn chairs he had loaned Stu for the star-watch the night before.

While Drew and Stu loaded the chairs into Drew's car, Angelica sat on the steps of the porch and pouted.

She was angry because her wish was taking so long to come true. Of course, she knew that sometimes you had to wait. After all, she'd had three whole birthdays already, so there were lots of wishes she'd made that were still on hold. But they were on hold for a very good reason: When those wishes came true, she would need a valid driver's license in order to use them.

The wish she had made the night before—her shooting star wish—wasn't like that, though. It shouldn't have taken very long. Wasn't the wish magic of a shooting star stronger than that of birthday candles?

And this time was even better. Instead of just her wish coming true, Angelica was going to get the babies' wishes too! Angelica laughed at the thought, then frowned again when she remembered her wish. Sigh! All she'd asked for was—

"ARRRRRR!"

Angelica screamed and whirled around.

Tommy and Chuckie stood in the open doorway holding Talking Reptar and giggling.

"You little monsters!" Angelica shouted. "You scared Cynthia!"

She started to stomp off.

"Wait, Angelica!" Tommy said. "We're sorry. Come back. We have a very important question to ask you."

Suddenly Angelica smiled. She found it hard to resist a question. It was a chance to show how smart she was.

"Okay, just one," she said. "What is it?"

"We want to know how long we have to wait before we get our wishes,"

Tommy said. Chuckie nodded.

Angelica's face turned beet red. She'd just been wondering and worrying the same thing about her own wish!

"What are you trying to say? That you don't believe me?" Angelica demanded.

"No, Angelica, honest," Chuckie said quickly.

"Well, you'll be sorry when you see what I wished for—and you didn't," she said. "I thought of the most bestest wish in the whole wide world!"

Tommy and Chuckie looked at one another and shrugged.

"Well?" Angelica snapped. "Don't you want to ask me what I wished for? Aren't you just dying to know?"

Tommy and Chuckie looked at Angelica and shrugged.

"It's against the rules to tell," she said, "but I'll give you a little hint. It starts

with 'm' and it ends with 'y' and it rhymes with 'honey,' and I'm gonna get lots and lots and lots of it!"

Tommy and Chuckie had no idea what she was talking about. They couldn't spell.

"*Rrrr!*" Angelica growled. She wanted them to be jealous. "Just you wait!"

When Angelica was gone, Tommy and Chuckie went out into the backyard. They peeked through the fence into Phil and Lil's backyard.

The twins were making identical castles in their backyard sandbox.

Tommy whispered, "Hey! Did you guys get any wishes yet?"

"Nah," Phil said. "The whole thing is like baloney."

"Yeah," Lil complained. "We want our money back!"

"But it didn't cost anything," Tommy said.

"Yeah, well, it's still not fair," Lil said. "We was really countin' on gettin' some big snakes."

"You're not supposed to say it!" Tommy cried. "Or it won't come true!"

"Who cares?" Phil said. "We might not find enough food to feed the big snakes, anyway."

"But, guys, we asked Angelica," Tommy told them, "and she said, 'Just you wait.' I think she means it's going to happen really soon!"

Suddenly they heard a baby cry. Chuckie's heart skipped a beat. Could it be? His wish had come true!

"Mine is the firstest one!" he cried. Tommy and Chuckie ran to the sound. It came from inside Tommy's house! The only thing between him and his new baby brother was Tommy.

"Look out, I'm comin' around!" Chuckie yelled, trying to pass Tommy.

"Hey," Tommy said. "Slow down, Chuckie! He's *my* brother!"

Chuckie stopped. "Oh, that was Baby Dil," he said. His shoulders sagged, and his glasses slid down his nose. "Sorry, Tommy."

Of course that was Tommy's baby brother and not *his* baby brother—the one who was coming from the shooting star. The one he couldn't tell Tommy about.

Chuckie followed Tommy slowly into the house. Baby Dil had stopped crying. He was drinking milk from a bottle in Didi's arms.

Tommy crawled up onto his mother's lap. He poked Dil's tummy with his

finger. He giggled as Dil grasped hold of his finger and smiled.

They looked so happy. Chuckie felt sad. Would his wish ever come true?

Chapter 6

Chuckie was playing in the backyard when someone yelled, "Hey, Chuckie! Whadda ya think of this baby!"

It was Tommy's grandpa, Lou. He was in Chuckie's backyard with Chas, Chuckie's dad.

"Huh?" Chuckie jumped to his feet and looked around. Did Grandpa Lou say, "baby"?

Chuckie couldn't see at first what Grandpa Lou was holding. But his dad looked really amazed.

Did Grandpa Lou find his baby brother? He ran up to the grown-ups to see.

But Grandpa Lou wasn't holding a baby. Instead he was holding up a huge red tomato. He had brought a whole basket of them to share with everyone. "Fresh from the garden!" he told Chuckie and his dad. "Grew these babies from seed!"

"Thanks, Lou," Chas said. "Chuckie and I will have this one for supper."

"Have some more!" Grandpa Lou said. "I grew so many tomatoes this year, I can't stand the sight of 'em!"

Back in his room Chuckie played alone. He took out a ball and played catch—just him and the wall.

"It's kind of lonely around here, huh, Reptar?" he said to the big lizard on his toy shelf. "I mean, Tommy has Dil, and Phil has Lil, and Angelica . . . Angelica has Cynthia. But what about *me?*"

He squeezed the toy's stomach, and it went, "AARRRRRR!"

"That's what you always say," Chuckie said sadly.

Then Chuckie spread out on the floor with paper and some crayons and drew a picture. It was a picture of himself, standing in front of his house. He colored in green trees, green grass, pink and purple flowers, and a big yellow sun.

He'd drawn this picture many times before. But this time he made it a little different. He added a baby

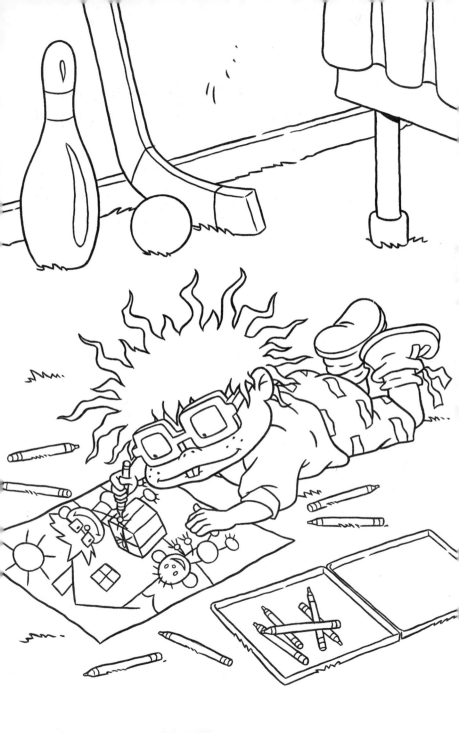

brother to the picture.

He imagined in the picture that it was his little brother's birthday. Then Chuckie drew in a present between the two of them in the drawing. He was giving his new brother a birthday present!

Suddenly Chuckie stopped drawing. "Maybe that's why my little brother isn't borned yet! He can't be borned till I get him a birthday present!"

Chapter 7

Chuckie never had a problem coming up with just the right present for his dad or his friends. Rocks, sticks, bugs . . . the world was full of wonderful things to share.

But this time Chuckie was having trouble.

Because this time the present was for a baby—a little baby.

You can't give a tiny baby rocks,

sticks, or bugs, Chuckie thought.

"A baby needs a real toy, Reptar," Chuckie said. "That's why I'm going to give him something of mine."

Chuckie went through everything in his toy box, scattering things all around the room. Nothing seemed right. He checked his shelves—nothing there, either.

He looked under his bed—nothing there but dust bunnies.

He checked his dresser drawers next. But they were full of clothes that were all too big for a new baby.

Chuckie lay back on the carpet with his fingers crisscrossed under his head. It reminded him of the night at the lake, looking up at the stars.

Then he spotted his Talking Reptar. It really was the best toy ever. And it would make a wonderful present for his new baby brother.

"Arrr . . . con-gradugation, Reptar!" Chuckie said as he stuffed the toy into his backpack. "And don't worry, 'cause you won't have to be in there too long. Like Angelica said, 'Just you wait!' "

Chapter 8

Chuckie waited. And waited. He waited all day for his new baby brother. But the only "baby" that came to Chuckie's house all day was Grandpa Lou's tomato at supper.

"Mmm . . . boy," Chas said. "This baby's delicious, isn't it, Chuckie?"

Chuckie nodded. But it was not a baby brother. Just then the phone rang. "Sounds great," Chas said when he

picked up the phone. "We'll be there!"

Maybe it was the baby store! Maybe they were supposed to pick up his baby brother now!

Chas hung up the phone and turned to Chuckie. "Come on, Chuckie," he said. "We're going over to Tommy's house for some homemade ice cream! Isn't that great?"

Chuckie smiled. Not as great as having a baby brother, he thought. Then he grabbed his backpack, and they headed out the door.

"Wanna play Reptar?" Tommy said when Chuckie got to his house. Chuckie looked around for any sign of a baby brother. But the only baby there was Dil.

Chuckie shrugged. "I guess so."

He tried to roar. *"Roar. Gr . . ."* But he

just didn't feel like it.

"What's wrong?" Tommy said.

"Nothin'," Chuckie said. Out Tommy's window he saw day fading slowly into night.

"You're thinkin' about your wish, huh, Chuckie?" Tommy guessed.

Chuckie nodded. "The whole day is almost over, and I haven't gotten my wish. . . . Have you?"

"Nope," said Tommy.

"Angelica said the first star was lucky. What if we didn't get to the lake in time for the lucky star? What if we were wishing on a star after the lucky star?"

"The UN-lucky star!" Chuckie said.

"Yeah, I bet there are lots and lotsa those!"

"Zillions!"

"Zillion billion gajillions!" Tommy said.

"I don't think we're gonna get the

wishes after all," Chuckie said.

Tommy sighed. "Then I guess it's okay to *spell* the beans."

"I guess," Chuckie said.

Chapter 9

"I wished for a baby brother," Chuckie told his friend. "Just like you have."

"Like Dil?" Tommy said, surprised. "I didn't know you wanted a baby brother."

"I didn't know, either," Chuckie said. "Until the shooting star came. Then my wish just sort of came out by itself."

Tommy took Chuckie's hand, and they walked over to Dil.

Dil gargled at him.

"Chuckie, meet your new baby brother," Tommy said. "Dil, this is Chuckie. Your new big brother."

Dil drooled.

"Wait, Tommy!" Chuckie gasped. "Dil can't be my little brother. He's already yours!"

"That's okay," Tommy said. "Lots of babies have more than one big brother. Dil can stay my little brother and be your little brother too."

Chuckie was shocked. It never occurred to him that a baby could have *two* big brothers.

"Do you think it'll be okay with your mommy and daddy?" Chuckie asked.

"Of course," Tommy said. "Now Dil will have two big brothers to look after him. So he'll be extra safe!"

"Gee, thanks, Tommy!" Chuckie said as he gave Dil a hug. "I got my wish!"

Then he remembered Tommy. "But

what about your wish?" Chuckie asked.

"It doesn't matter," Tommy said.

"You're gonna get your wish too, Tommy," Chuckie told him.

"How do you know?" Tommy said. "You don't even know what my wish was."

"Yes, I do," Chuckie said. Then he opened his backpack and handed the present to Tommy.

"Talking Reptar?" Tommy gasped. "But this is yours!"

Chuckie grinned. "If you can share Dil, then I can share Reptar, too!" he said.

Tommy smiled. He squeezed Reptar's tummy.

"ARRRR!" said Reptar.

"ARRRR!" said Tommy, and Chuckie, and Baby Dil.

About the Authors

Do wishes come true? **Cathy East Dubowski** and **Mark Dubowski** know that some do, because their big wish came true—to write and illustrate books for children. Over the years the creative husband and wife team have written and illustrated dozens of books, including many featuring licensed characters.

By day Mark and Cathy work in a pair of old barns near their home. At night they watch the stars with their daughters, Lauren and Megan, and their two golden retrievers, Macdougal and Morgan, at their home in Chapel Hill, North Carolina.